SONG AND DANCE MAN

SONG AND DANCE MAN

by KAREN ACKERMAN

illustrated by STEPHEN GAMMELL

Dragonfly Books ———— New York

Grandpa was a song and dance man who once danced on the vaudeville stage.

When we visit, he tells us about a time before people watched TV, back in the good old days, the song and dance days.

"Supper in an hour!" Grandma calls from the kitchen.

"I wonder if my tap shoes still fit?" Grandpa says with a smile. Then he turns on the light to the attic, and we follow him up the steep, wooden steps.

Faded posters of Grandpa when he was young hang on
the walls. He moves some cardboard boxes and a rack of
Grandma's winter dresses out of the way, and we see a
dusty brown, leather-trimmed trunk in the corner.

As soon as Grandpa opens it, the smell of cedar chips and old things saved fills the attic. Inside are his shoes with the silver, half-moon taps on the toes and heels, bowler hats and top hats, and vests with stripes and matching bow ties.

We try on the hats and pretend we're dancing on a vaudeville stage, where the bright lights twinkle and the piano player nods his head along with the music.

After wiping his shoes with a cloth he calls a shammy, Grandpa puts them on. He tucks small, white pads inside the shoes so his corns won't rub, and he turns on the lamps and aims each one down like a spotlight.

He sprinkles a little powder on the floor, and it's show time.
We sit on one of Grandma's woolen blankets, clap our hands,
and call out, "Yay, Grandpa!"

The song and dance man begins to dance the old soft
shoe. His feet move slowly at first, while his tap shoes make
soft, slippery sounds like rain on a tin roof.
    We forget that it's Grandpa dancing, and all we can hear
is the silvery tap of two feet, and all we can see is a song
and dance man gliding across a vaudeville stage.

He says, "Watch this!" and does a new step that sounds like a woodpecker tapping on a tree. Suddenly, his shoes move faster, and he begins to sing. His voice is as round and strong as a canyon echo, and his cheeks get rosy as he sings "Yankee Doodle Boy," a song he knows from the good old days.

There are too many dance steps and too many words in the song for us to remember, but the show is better than any show on TV.

The song and dance man stops and leans forward with a wink.

"What's that in your ear?" he asks, and he pulls a silver dollar out of somebody's hair.

He rolls his bowler hat down his arm, catches it in his hand, and flips it back up onto his head.

"Know how to make an elephant float?" he asks. "One scoop of ice cream, two squirts of soda, and three scoops of elephant!" We've heard that joke before, but the song and dance man slaps his knee and laughs until his eyes water.

He tries to wipe them with a red hanky from his vest pocket, but the hanky just gets longer and longer as he pulls it out. He looks so surprised that we start laughing too, and it feels like the whole attic is shaking.

Sometimes we laugh so hard, the hiccups start, and
Grandpa stops to bring us a glass of water from the
bathroom.

"Drink slow and hold your breath," he says, "or I'll have
to scare you!"

Once our hiccups are gone, he gets a gold-tipped cane
and a black silk top hat from the trunk. He lowers his eyes
and tips the hat, and he's standing very still.

All the lights are turned low except one that shines on his
polished tap shoes. It's the grand finale, so the song and
dance man takes a deep breath. He lifts the cane and holds
it in both hands.

Slowly, he starts to tap. His shoes move faster and faster, and the sounds coming from them are too many to make with only two feet.

He spins and jumps into the air. Touching the stage again, he kneels with his arms spread out, and the silk top hat and gold-tipped cane lie side by side at his feet. His shoes are still, and the show is over.

We stand up together and clap our hands, shouting
"Hurray!" and "More!" but Grandpa only smiles and shakes
his head, all out of breath. He takes off his tap shoes, wraps
them gently in the shammy cloth, and puts them back in
the leather-trimmed trunk. He carefully folds his vest
and lays the top hat and cane on it, and we follow him to
the stairway.

Grandpa holds on to the rail as we go down the steps.
At the bottom he hugs us, and we tell him we wish we
could have seen him dance in the good old days, the song
and dance days. He smiles, and whispers that he wouldn't
trade a million good old days for the days he spends with us.

But as he turns off the attic light, Grandpa glances back up the stairs, and we wonder how much he really misses that time on the vaudeville stage, when he was a song and dance man.

For Shoshi, Ari, and Avi—
and for my father, Morry,
who loved to waltz
—K. A.

Text copyright © 1988 by Karen Ackerman
Illustrations copyright © 1988 by Stephen Gammell

Visit us on the Web! www.randomhouse.com/kids

Educators and librarians, for a variety of teaching tools, visit us at www.randomhouse.com/teachers

The Library of Congress has cataloged the hardcover edition of this work as follows:

Ackerman, Karen. / Song and dance man.
Summary: Grandpa demonstrates for his visiting grandchildren some of the songs,
dances, and jokes he performed when he was a vaudeville entertainer.
ISBN 978-0-394-89330-3 (trade) — ISBN 978-0-394-99330-0 (lib. bdg.)
[1. Entertainers—Fiction. 2. Grandfathers—Fiction.]
I. Gammell, Stephen, ill. II. Title.
PZ7.A1824So   1988   [E]   87003200

ISBN 978-0-679-81995-0 (pbk.)

MANUFACTURED IN CHINA

40